Madeline's Rescue

MADELINE'S RESCUE

Story and pictures by

Ludwig Bemelmans

PUFFIN BOOKS

PUFFIN BOOKS
Published by the Penguin Group
Viking Penguin Inc., 40 West 23rd Street, New York, New York 10010, U.S.A.
Penguin Books Ltd, 27 Wrights Lane, London W8 5TZ England
Penguin Books Australia Ltd, Ringwood, Victoria, Australia
Penguin Books Canada Ltd, 2801 John Street, Markham, Ontario, Canada L3R 1B4
Penguin Books (N.Z.) Ltd, 182–190 Wairau Road, Auckland 10, New Zealand

Penguin Books Ltd, Registered Offices: Harmondsworth, Middlesex, England

First published by The Viking Press 1953
Viking Seafarer Edition published 1973
Reprinted 1975
Published in Picture Puffins 1977
15 17 19 20 18 16 14

Library of Congress Cataloging in Publication Data
Bemelmans, Ludwig, 1898–1962. Madeline's rescue.
Summary: A hound rescues Madeline from the
Seine, becomes a beloved school pet, is chased away
by the trustees, and returns with a surprise.
[1. Dogs—Fiction. 2. Paris—Fiction.
3. Stories in rhyme] I. Title.
PZ8.3.B425 Mah12 [E] 77-2573
ISBN 0-14-050207-6

Manufactured in the U.S.A.

Set in Bodoni

Madeline's Rescue

In an old house in Paris that was covered with vines
Lived twelve little girls in two straight lines.
They left the house at half past nine
In two straight lines in rain or shine.
The smallest one was Madeline.
She was not afraid of mice.
She loved winter, snow, and ice.
To the tiger in the zoo
Madeline just said, "Pooh pooh!"

And nobody knew so well
How to frighten Miss Clavel—

Until the day she slipped and fell.

Poor Madeline would now be dead

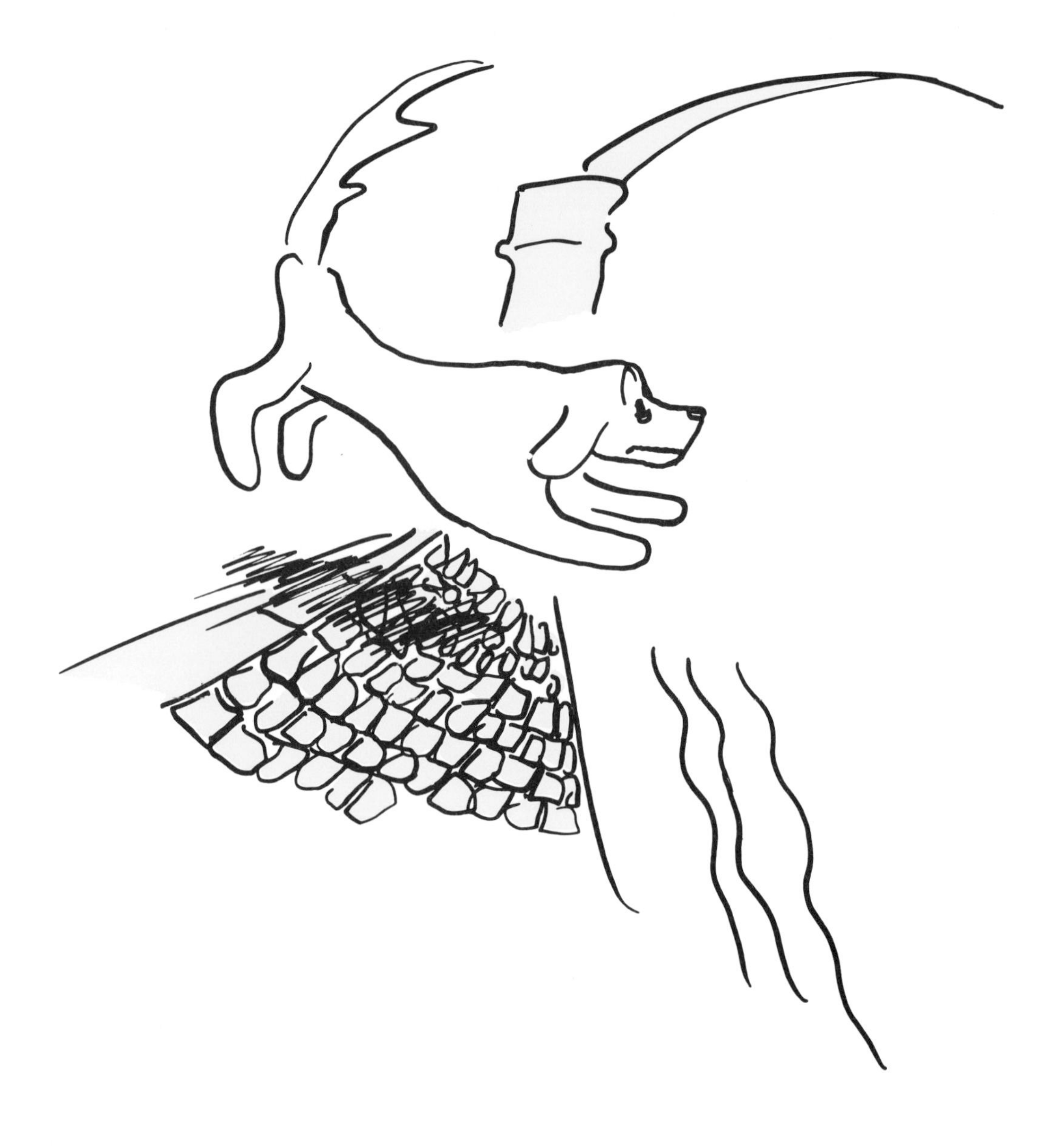

But for a dog

That kept its head,

And dragged her safe from a watery grave.

INSTITUT DE FRANCE

"From now on, I hope you will listen to me,

“And here is a cup of camomile tea.

"Good night, little girls—I hope you sleep well."
"Good night, good night, dear Miss Clavel!"

Miss Clavel turned out the light.
After she left there was a fight
About where the dog should sleep that night.

The new pupil was ever
So helpful and clever.

The dog loved biscuits, milk, and beef
And they named it Genevieve.

She could sing and almost talk

And enjoyed the daily walk.

Soon the snow began to fly,
Inside it was warm and dry
And six months passed quickly by.

When the first of May came near
There was nervousness each year.

For on that day there arrived a collection
Of trustees for the annual inspection.

The inspection was most thorough,
Much to everybody's sorrow.

"Tap, tap!" "Whatever can that be?"
"Tap, tap!" "Come out and let me see!
"Dear me, it's a dog! Isn't there a rule
"That says DOGS AREN'T ALLOWED IN SCHOOL?"

“Miss Clavel, get rid of it, please,”
Said the president of the board of trustees.
“Yes, but the children love her so,”
Said Miss Clavel. “Please don’t make her go.”

"I daresay," said Lord Cucuface.
"I mean—it's a perfect disgrace
"For young ladies to embrace
"This creature of uncertain race!

"Off with you! Go on—run! scat!
"Go away and don't come back!"

Madeline jumped on a chair.
"Lord Cucuface," she cried, "beware!
"Miss Genevieve, noblest dog in France,
"You shall have your VEN-GE-ANCE!"

"It's no use crying or talking.
"Let's get dressed and go out walking.
"The sooner we're ready, the sooner we'll leave—
"The sooner we'll find Miss Genevieve."

They went looking high

and low

And every place a dog might go.

In every place they called her name

But no one answered to the same.

The gendarmes said, "We don't believe
"We've seen a dog like Genevieve."

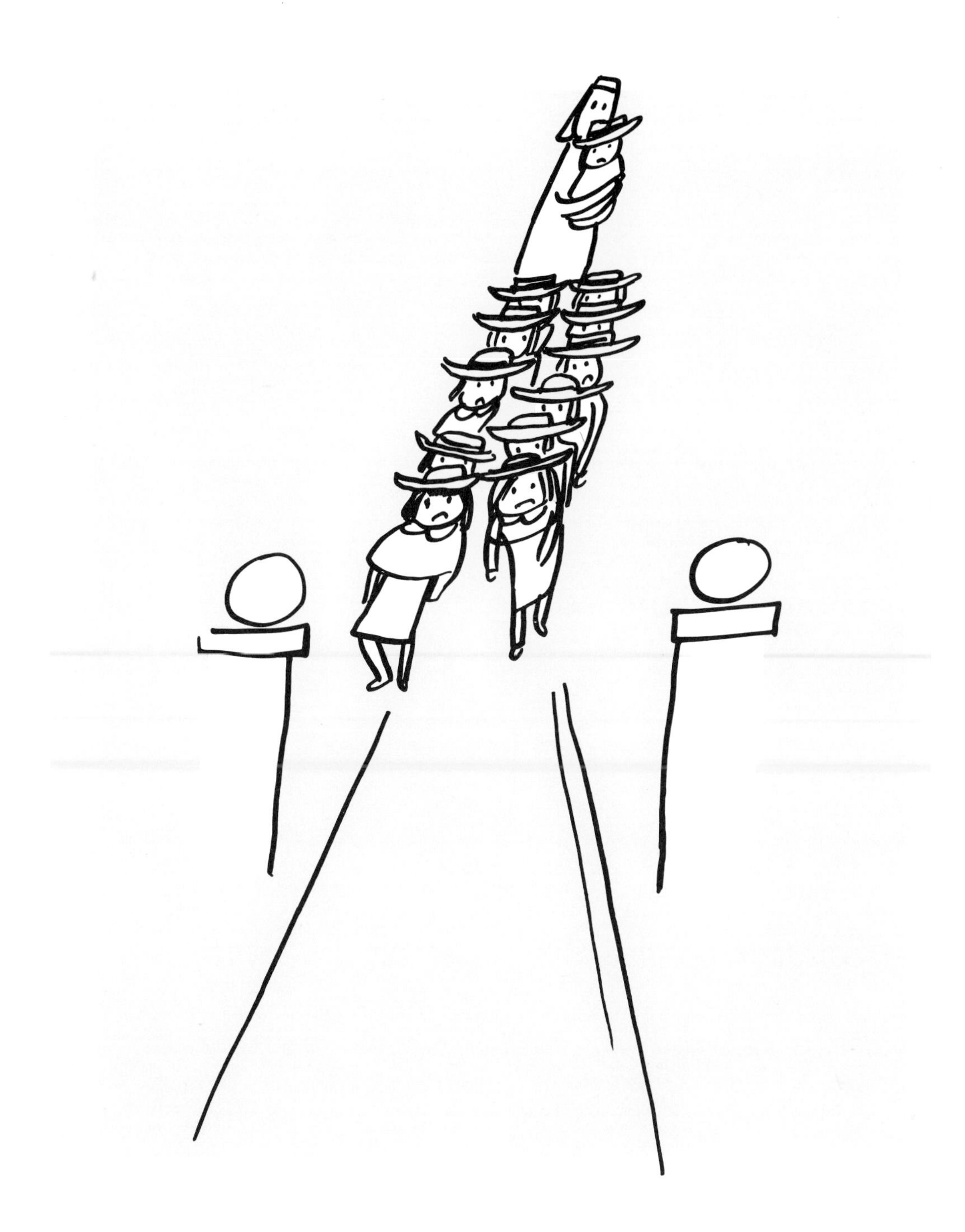

Hours after they had started
They came back home broken-hearted.

"Oh, Genevieve, where can you be?
"Genevieve, please come back to me."

In the middle of the night
Miss Clavel turned on the light.
And said, "Something is not right."

An old street lamp shed its light
On Miss Genevieve outside.

She was petted, she was fed,
And everybody went to bed.

"Good night, little girls, I hope you sleep well."
"Good night, good night, dear Miss Clavel!"

Miss Clavel turned out the light,
And again there was a fight,
As each little girl cried,
"Genevieve is *mine* tonight!"

For a second time that night
Miss Clavel turned on her light,

And afraid of a disaster,
She ran fast—

And even faster.

"If there's one more fight about Genevieve,
"I'm sorry, but she'll have to leave!"

That was the end of the riot—
Suddenly all was quiet.

For the third time that night
Miss Clavel turned on the light,

And to her surprise she found

That suddenly there was enough hound

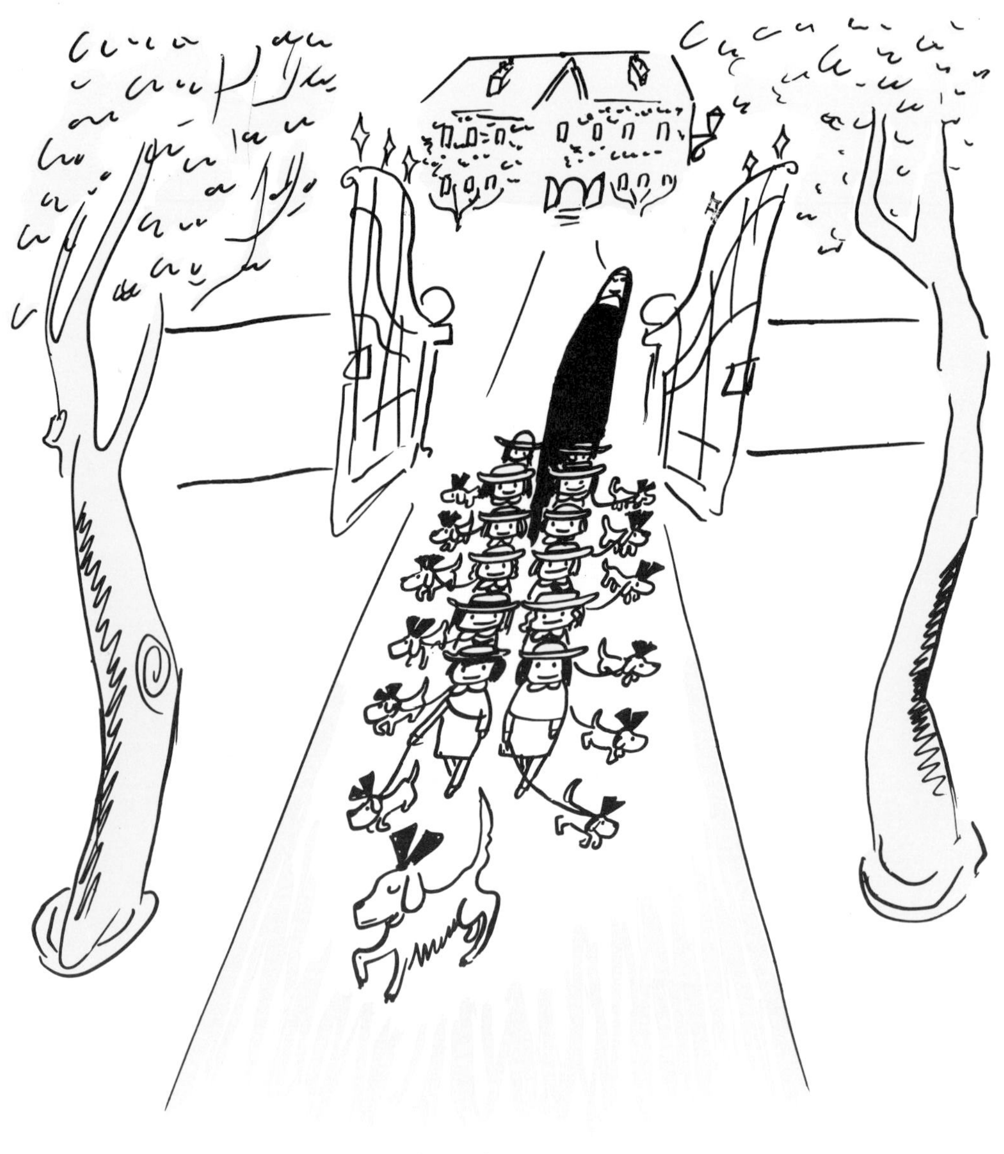

To go all around.